JULIE CHEN

WHEN I GROW UP

illustrated by DIANE GOODE

A PAULA WISEMAN BOOK

Simon & Schuster Books for Young Readers

New York • London • Toronto • Sydney • New Delhi

SIMON & SCHUSTER BOOKS FOR YOUNG READERS • An imprint of Simon & Schuster Children's Publishing Division • 1230 Avenue of the Americas, New York, New York 10020 • Text copyright © 2018 by Julie Chen • Illustrations copyright © 2018 by Diane Goode • All rights reserved, including the right of reproduction in whole or in part in any form. • SIMON & SCHUSTER BOOKS FOR YOUNG READERS is a trademark of Simon & Schuster, Inc. • For information about special discounts for bulk purchases, please contact Simon & Schuster Special Sales at 1-866-506-1949 or business@simonandschuster.com. • The Simon & Schuster Speakers Bureau can bring authors to your live event. For more information or to book an event, contact the Simon & Schuster Speakers Bureau at 1-866-248-3049 or visit our website at www.simonspeakers.com. • Book design by Jessica Handelman • The text for this book was set in Tribute. • The illustrations for this book were rendered in watercolor. • Manufactured in China • 0718 SCP • First Edition • 10 9 8 7 6 5 4 3 2 1 • Library of Congress Cataloging-in-Publication Data • Names: Chen, Julie, author. | Goode, Diane, illustrator. • Title: When I grow up / Julie Chen ; illustrated by Diane Goode. • Description: First edition. | New York : Simon & Schuster Books for Young Readers, [2018] | "A Paula Wiseman Book." | Summary: When a young boy imagines what he might be and do one day, his mother assures him that he can be anything, and she will always be there for him. • Identifiers: LCCN 2018000597| ISBN 9781481497190 (hardcover) | ISBN 9781481497206 (e-book) • Subjects: | CYAC: Occupations—Fiction. | Mother and child—Fiction. | Bedtime—Fiction. • Classification: LCC PZ7.1.C4973 Whe 2018 | DDC [E]—dc23 LC record available at https://lccn.loc.gov/2018000597

To my son, Charlie:
You will accomplish all your good wishes in life!—J. C.

For my son—D. G.

Mom, when I grow up,
what do you think I will be?

Will I be funny or smart?

Do you think I'll live near or far?

Will I be a baker
and make the world a sweeter place to live?

Will I be a teacher
and let dogs come to school?

Will I be a writer
and tell stories of places faraway and long ago?

Will I be the mayor
and let kids run the town?

Will I be a climber
and reach the mountaintops?

Will I be a gardener
and plant seeds all around and watch them grow?

Will I be an astronaut
and see the world from afar?

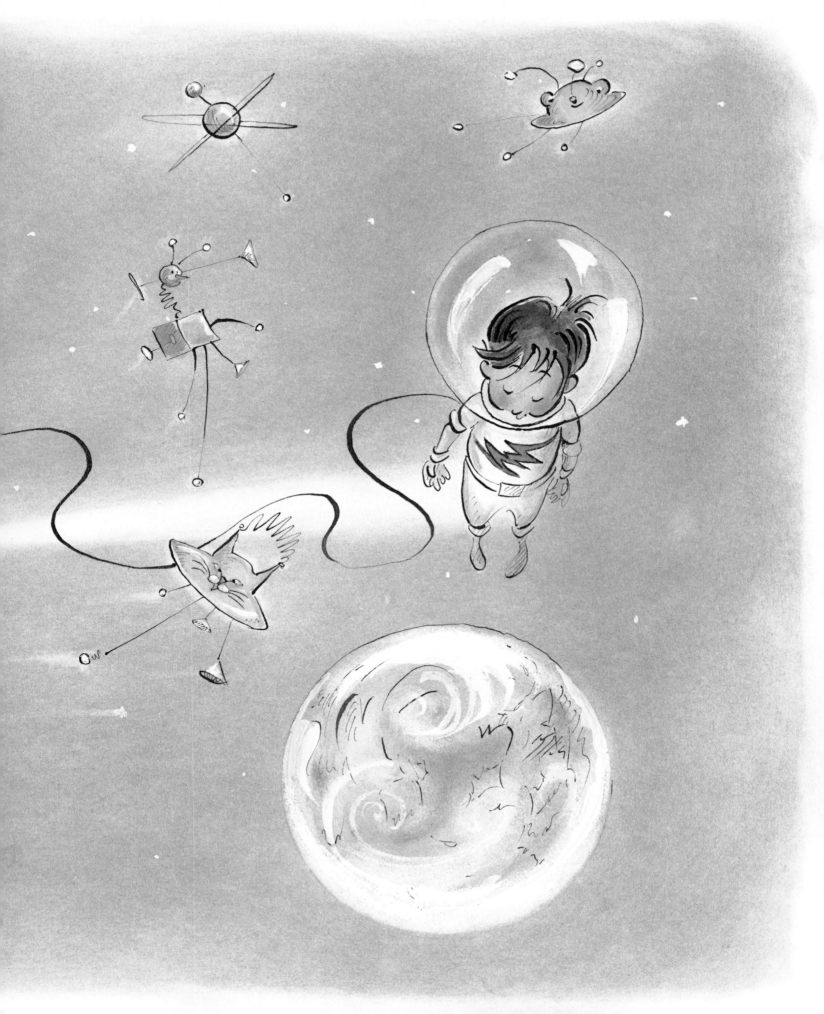

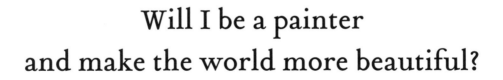

Will I be a painter
and make the world more beautiful?

Will I be a builder
and watch my buildings touch the sky?

Will I be a musician
and fill the world with lovely sounds?

Mom, I can't wait to grow up.

When you grow up,
you can be whatever you dream.

No matter what,
I will always be there for you.
Just like now. I'll always hold on.

Let's dream of tomorrow together.